Dedication

This book is dedicated:

To Ernst ... My wonderful husband, friend, knight-in-shining-armor, and forever the love of my life ...

To Ryan ... My super son, friend, messenger-of-mirth, and forever my golden child ...

To Katy ... My darling daughter, friend, commander-of-courage, and forever my rainbow child ...

To Elsie ... My precious mother, friend, mentor-of-rhyme, and forever my role model ...

And also,

In memory of Robert ... My beloved father, friend, guardian angel, and forever my true hero!

Acknowledgments

This book would never have been written if it hadn't been for the encouragement of my dear friend and former teaching partner, Janet Georgas. Not only did she insist that I could and should write a children's book in rhyme, but she backed up her belief in me by doing all the typing and editing! Janet, a simple thank you is not enough, but I hope you know that you have my gratitude and friendship always!

It took only one meeting at Starbucks for me to realize that Ellen Berger, another teaching colleague, was the perfect illustrator for this book. She visualized not only the spirit of the book, but captured both the scenes and characters that roamed through my head. Thank you, Ellen, for delightfully enhancing my stories with your beautiful artwork, and for sharing the excitement of creating this book!

My daughter, Katy, continued to breathe courage into me every step of the way during this lengthy project. Perhaps even more importantly, she bought me an extraordinary birthday gift, with which I wrote every single word of this text. On a trip to Mt. Vernon together, she purchased a pen for me, crafted from the wood of actual trees planted by George Washington on his plantation more than two centuries ago. Writing with that particular instrument was inspiring, and a little like taking a trip back in time. Thank you, Katy, for my "Magic Pen"!

In addition to his marketing advice, my son, Ryan, provided me with countless moments of laughter and helped me keep this project in perspective. Thanks, Ryan, for always being there for me!

From cover to cover, *Patriotic Pups* was made possible because of the total commitment and support of my husband, Ernst. On several vacations we made, he patiently took scores of pictures of various places mentioned in this book, and he continues to manage all of the business required in such an endeavor. Thank you, Ernie, for always helping to make my dreams come true!

Table of Contents

- The Legend Begins -

(1774)

As the morning mist rose from the river
Peter quickened his steps as he sought to deliver
Some happy news of a special event;
So special, in fact, he knew that it meant
Mr. Washington would forego his breakfast to see
The litter of pups born at half past three.
Upon hearing the news, George grabbed his hat,
And donned his boots in ten seconds flat!

Lady Liberty's pups were a rowdy litter –
Ears all floppy and tails atwitter.
They sniffed and rolled all over the stable
And ran through the yard as soon as they were able.
They chewed on boots and chased their tails,
Bumping into churns and turning over pails.
The pups, like their mother, were gentle and sweet,
And no happier pups would you ever meet.

Rebel, their papa, was a champion sire,
And the puppies inherited his courage and fire.
His instinct for hunting and his loyal heart
Were seen in those puppies from the very start.
Their spirits were bold, and their senses keen,
And no finer pups had George Washington seen.
As they grew, he gave each one a name,
Never guessing then they'd one day know fame!

At two months of age, their lessons began,
They learned obedience and tracking, they jumped and they ran.
Before long, their first birthday came 'round,
And George knew that it was time that he found
For each young dog, a happy new place,
With a master just waiting for a loveable face.
His pups would be given to special friends –
And so, this is how each story begins …

Beacon

George whistled low for Beacon to come,
And Beacon's fast response made George's spirits hum.
For George knew that Beacon would need to be quick
To live with the Patriot he'd decided to pick
As the master of this loveable pet –
A choice George knew he'd never regret.

So into the carriage for a long, long ride
Went Beacon, with George close at his side.
The road to Boston was dusty and rough.
And just when Beacon had had quite enough,
The carriage stopped as a rider drew near,
Then down from his saddle stepped Paul Revere.

He shook George's hand, and patted Beacon's head.
"Why George, what a fine dog," he eagerly said.
"I've need of a friend to stay close at hand,
Guiding and guarding as I ride o'er the land.
I thank you well for a gift such as this.
He's a champion whose company I'd not want to miss."

BOSTON

MT. VERNON

ATLANTIC OCEAN

Kite

The warm spring wind blew his huge ears high,
Making everyone laugh when the pup ran by.
His run up a hill was more flight than game,
And it was those flying ears that gave him his name.
"I'll call him Kite," said George with a smile,
Knowing that this lively pup would be just the style
For a friend and Patriot he'd had in mind –
A master for Kite who'd be loving and kind.

A few weeks later when Philadelphia came into view
Somehow George Washington instinctively knew
That a dog as clever and amusing as Kite
Was the perfect pet, and would be just right
For a friend whose inventions had brought him fame –
His Patriot friend, Ben Franklin by name.

Kite and Ben would share great times together,
Wherever they went, whatever the weather.
So, George was happy as he rode out of sight,
Knowing Ben Franklin would always love Kite.

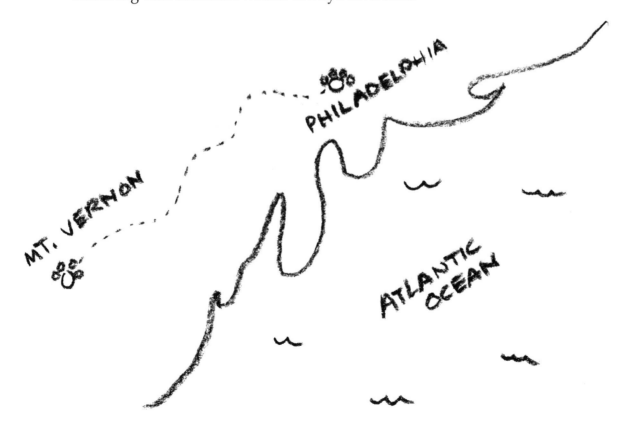

Quill

Rolling up the parchment, George had to smile,
Because at his feet, all the while,
Quill had slept as George worked away,
Bringing calm and comfort to the stormy day.
His gentle nature and desire to please
Helped George make his decision with the utmost of ease.
A Patriot he knew who was thoughtful and mellow,
Would welcome Quill at his home, Monticello.

So George saddled a steed, and bade Quill to follow,
And began a journey through dale and hollow,
To a mountaintop house his friend called home,
A place so unique its roof was a dome.
His friend was a scholar, creative, and kind,
A man with a most remarkable mind.
Thomas Jefferson and Quill would be a perfect pair,
And George knew that the two would surely share
The bond of friendship so loyal and true,
That it's only given to a special few.

And George's hunch was certainly right,
For Quill and Tom made quite a sight
As they greeted each other like friends old and dear,
Whose time together would bring nothing but cheer.
Quill's tail was wagging to beat the band,
As he roamed and explored Tom's mountaintop land.
So with the coming of the morning light,
George headed for home with the plan he thought right,
For the one last pup he needed to place –
The beagle whose smile never left his face.

Banner

With adoring eyes and wagging tail,
Banner's loving ways could never fail
To bring sunshine into any room,
Banishing sadness and discouraging gloom.
And though by nature he was jolly and warm,
Banner would protect if someone meant harm
To those he loved, or even a stranger,
For Banner was a master at sensing danger.

George Washington thought of a Patriot he knew,
Whose loyalties and courage were always true blue.
He knew she'd need Banner's comic ways
To ease the strain of the coming days,
And guard her in the dark of night;
Yes, he knew his Banner would be just right!

So, one last journey George decided to make,
All for the cause, and his good friend's sake.
To Philadelphia he'd travel once more,
And knock upon this Patriot's door.
George was certain and willing to bet,
That Mrs. Betsy Ross would adore this pet!

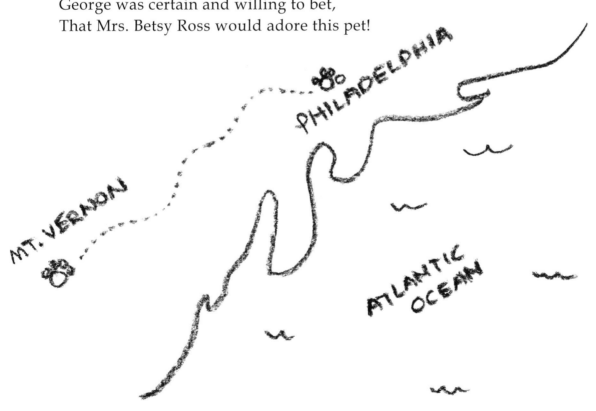

1775

With the last pup placed in capable hands
Washington knew 'twas time to face the army's demands.
So, kissing Martha and hugging her tight
He whistled for Rebel, and they rode out of sight.

He'd left Lady Liberty to help Martha smile
As he and Rebel rode mile after mile
To take command of the coming fights,
Against King George, who'd taken the rights
From his loyal subjects across the sea,
Giving them cause to fight to be free!

Leaving his home that bleak, dreary day,
Washington wondered if they'd find a way
To convince the King and Parliament
That the colonists, who constantly sent
Messages seeking their own true rights,
Were not beyond bloodshed and fights.

He thought of all the Patriots he knew,
Who knew for certain what they must do,
And of the pups he'd given away,
To protect those Patriots every day.
He wondered where it all would lead …

… And you'll find out if you continue to read!

- Beacon -

(April 1775)

In his silversmith's shop stood Paul Revere,
Who smiled at the dog sleeping peacefully near.
The hour grew late, and they'd soon need to go,
To spread the warning other Patriots must know.
Paul needed Beacon for a guard and a guide,
As he attempted to make this important ride.

Beacon's eyes and ears were exceptionally keen
And Paul knew that the ride toward Lexington Green
Would be filled with darkness and danger, too,
So he'd need Beacon's help getting the message through.
But just for now he'd let Beacon rest,
To gain his strength for the coming test.

When the clock struck twelve, Paul whistled low,
Signaling Beacon it was time to go.
While saddling his horse at this midnight hour,
Paul kept his eyes on the North Church tower.
And all this time Beacon stood ready to run,
Sensing something important had just begun.

When the tower's second light came into view,
Beacon tensed with excitement because he knew
That he and Paul must move with great speed,
So he took his place in front of Paul's steed,
And bounded off into the night,
To warn the Patriots of the coming fight.

The road proved rocky, and tore at his paws,
But on Beacon ran for the good of the cause.
"THE REDCOATS ARE COMING!" he barked loud and clear,
"Prepare to fight for the rights you hold dear!"
And as he barked, Paul shouted out loud,
Hoping the British would face quite a crowd.

His throat was dry, but his bark was strong,
As he woke the men to join in the throng
Of the sleepy farmers who prepared to die
When they heard his bark, and Paul's urgent cry:
"To arms, to arms! The British draw near!
They'll be at the green when sunrise is here!"

There were twists and turns in the road as they ran,
But Beacon's nose had been part of the plan.
So he sniffed at the air and led the way
As he sensed the danger of the coming day,
And thanks to that nose and his bark loud and clear,
The message was heard by all, far and near.

But Beacon's job was not done yet,
For as the moon had begun to set,
Some British soldiers stopped Paul on his way,
And it fell to Beacon to save the day!
He yipped and he snarled, and raised such a stir
That Paul and his horse escaped in a blur!

As Beacon followed, a shot rang out –
And missed him by inches, of that he'd no doubt.
But he caught up with Paul who beamed with pride,
At the Patriotic Pup close by his side.
The pup who had run mile after mile,
Now paused with Paul to rest for awhile.

The sky turned pink with the rising sun,
And Beacon's ear heard the sound of a gun.
The musket that fired the first shot that day
Was heard 'round the world, or so they say.
That shot had ignited a tiny spark,
Which soon caught fire, bringing light to the dark.

Though his legs were weary and his paws very sore,
Beacon rose to run with Paul once more.
But his master was wise and scooped Beacon up,
Placing across his saddle one tired pup.
Thus, Beacon rode back to Boston that day,
On a tall, black horse, sleeping all the way.

Through all the hard years of that terrible war
Beacon barked for freedom, and was never far
From that famous and historic messenger's side,
Who gave freedom its start with his midnight ride.
And Beacon the Bold, from Mount Vernon plantation,
Became a true Founding Pup of our brand new nation!

- Banner -

(1776)

Banner bounded after the spool of thread,
Banging the table, and bumping his head.
"What a scamp you are!" laughed Betsy Ross,
Patting his head, then giving the spool a toss.
"Since the General brought you it's been nothing but fun.
You're lively, and happy, and kind to everyone."
With a wag of his tail, he licked Betsy's hand.
Yes, life with this seamstress was really quite grand.

It was quite a surprise when a knock at the door
Brought the General to Betsy's home once more.
Banner leaped with excitement and howled with joy.
"Come," laughed the General, "Now, that's a good boy!"
The General sat by the fire while Betsy served tea.
"Sir, how goes the war to set us all free?"
Asked Betsy, who knew from Washington's frown,
That his mind was weary, and his spirits were down.

"Well Betsy, the troops are ill-trained and supplies are few.
That's why I've come to ask a favor of you.
Your skills are perfect to fulfill the need
Of designing a symbol to help us succeed.
My men need a banner, a flag of some kind
To lead them in battle as they march behind.
You'll know best how it should be made –
A flag fit for battle, or to march in a parade."

Giving Banner a quick pat on the head,
George thanked Betsy for the food he'd been fed.
Then, tipping his hat and donning his cloak,
He turned to Betsy and quietly spoke.
"Betsy, tell no one of this task that you do,
For helping our troops could bring danger to you.
Keep Banner nearby and your shutters closed tight.
Work on the flag only at night."

Bolting the door and giving Banner a wink,
Betsy got paper and pen, then sat down to think.
She made stars and stripes in designs of all hue.
She couldn't decide just what she should do.
So late into night Betsy worked and thought,
About all the reasons the Patriots fought.
They fought to speak freely, and make their own laws,
And Betsy was thrilled to be part of the cause!

All that night Betsy's thoughts fairly flew
And she thought she was certain the flag should be blue,
With thirteen stars in a circle of white.
But what other color would be just right?
Dousing the candles and longing for sleep,
She decided that question would just have to keep
Until morning came with dawn's early light,
When her mind would be clear and her ideas bright.

So Banner kept vigil while Betsy slept,
Always mindful that his promise be kept
Of seeing that Betsy had no cause to fear,
Even with the Redcoats camping near.
As the glowing embers in the firelight grew dim,
Banner knew it was entirely up to him
To keep Betsy safe and free from harm,
So, snuggling close all night, he kept her warm.

After breakfast, Betsy faced a new day,
And Banner barked that he wanted to play.
So they went for a walk in the downtown square
With Banner leaping at birds flying through the air.
Bounding up some steps, and avoiding a fall,
Banner's bark sharply gave out a call
To the beagle who peeked out the window sill –
Thomas Jefferson's dog, his own brother, Quill!

The brothers romped and playfully yipped,
As up and down the steps they zipped.
Then rounding the corner to their delight
They spotted Ben Franklin with their third brother, Kite.
He joined in their play all around the square
Causing the delegates to stop and stare.
Their antics erased the dark clouds that day,
Chasing the horrors of war far away.

The dogs had a jolly romp that day,
But knew it was time to end their play.
So they wagged their tails, and off they ran,
Returning to the homes where their day began.
But as Banner skidded and slid through the door,
He spied Betsy's sewing box on the floor.
It was all too late when he tried to stop
So he slammed into that box with a resounding "POP!"

Bright colored spools spun 'round his head,
Entangling him in yards of her thread.
Betsy came at once when she heard the commotion,
And spied the pup, as if in slow motion.
Betsy laughed and said, "Oh, silly you –
You're all bound up in red, white, and blue!"
And Banner made such a startling sight,
That Betsy knew the mixture would be just right.

When the General arrived to claim his treasure,
He knew that its worth was beyond all measure.
And he also knew that Banner the Bright
Had stayed by her side as she sewed through the night.
So, when you pledge allegiance to the red, white, and blue,
Remember this tale that's been told to you,
About Betsy's flag and the mirthful manner
Of her Patriotic Pup, the Star Spangled Banner!

- Quill -

(1775 - 1776)

A perfect place for a pup to roam
Was Monticello, Tom Jefferson's home.
Up on a mountain, amid tall, green trees,
Quill paused to sniff at the evening breeze.
The scent of his master caused Quill to run
To the house bathed in light from the setting sun.
So through the garden he zigged and he zagged,
With a bounding gait and a tail that wagged.

Approaching the house through the evening haze
Quill caught the glimpse of his master's gaze,
As he stood at the window in contemplation,
Wondering how to help his struggling nation.
"Ah, Quill," said Tom as the pup drew near,
"It's time we journeyed away from here.
The Pennsylvania State House is where we must go,
To meet with other Patriots I already know."

The room was noisy as each man came in,
But Quill waited quietly for it all to begin.
Ben Franklin's arrival was quite a sight,
Causing Quill to think of his brother, Kite,
Who'd gone to live, just last winter,
With Patriot Ben, the famous inventor.
When Franklin sat down in his delegated chair,
Quill felt electricity flow through the air.

Then in walked John Adams and John Hancock, too,
As well as some others that Jefferson knew.
Tom motioned for Quill to sit at his feet,
When suddenly, the gavel whacked out a beat,
Signaling all it was time to begin
The discussions about how they could possibly win
This war that grew greater with each passing day,
Filling all with fear, and much dismay.

The delegates argued, often loud and long.
They couldn't decide whether it was right or wrong
To demand the King take his Redcoats away
And recognize us as the U.S.A.
So they appointed a committee to make it clear
About the things the King should hear.
But whose pen would write the words of reason,
The words the King would consider treason?

To Thomas Jefferson fell this task,
"But why Mr. Jefferson?" you might ask.
He'd a way with words and the others knew
If anyone could get their message through,
It would be the Virginian and his mighty quill pen
That would convince the King and all his men
That the American people would not back down
To the King who wore that gold British crown!

With the State House only blocks away
Tom took Quill where they both would stay
In a house quite cozy, and really just right.
'Twas a perfect place to spend day and night
Composing a letter, a declaration,
Telling the King we'd formed a new nation,
And his rule over us was a thing of the past,
For we'd fight to the death to make our freedom last!

Tom ripped up the paper, then wadded it up,
Making a ball for his faithful pup.
He tried and he tried as days went by,
Writing, and rewriting, then giving a sigh.
The words must be clear, but powerful as well,
To explain the ideas the Patriots must sell,
So that all the people would join in the fight,
And so that the King would learn they were right.

Quill leaned his head on his master's knee,
Giving comfort for the distress he could see.
When night turned to morning and Tom couldn't rest,
It was Quill's gentle nature that soothed him the best.
When Quill pawed those paper balls tossed on the floor,
Tom would smile to himself and start writing once more.
And finally, at dawn on July the 1st,
From his house on the corner, Thomas Jefferson burst!

Tom ran to the State House, took John Adams aside,
Handed him the paper, and smiled with pride.
"It's the finest writing I've ever done,
But I've a sinking feeling our work's just begun."
All that day, and the next day, too,
The delegates argued 'til their faces were blue.
Yet, the evening of July 2nd they took a new vote
And all said "Yea" to the paper Tom wrote!

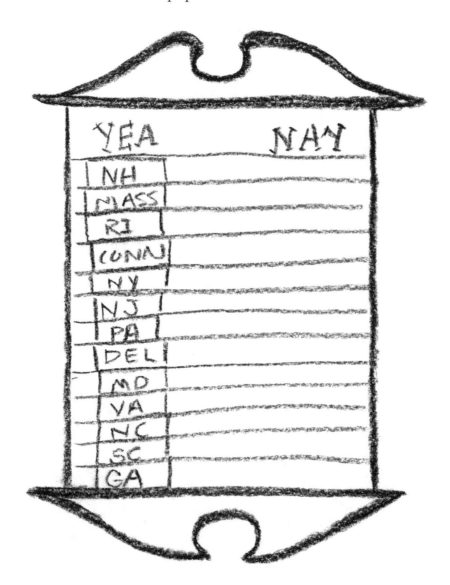

Quill sensed tension among them all
As each man stepped up when the clerk gave a call.
He watched with interest as each man signed his name,
And wagged his tail when Tom's turn came.
By signing their names on that paper they knew
If the Redcoats caught them their lives were through.
But they strongly believed that all men had rights
And the cause for freedom was clear in their sights.

Riders sped copies to the south and the north,
And as bells rang out on July the 4th,
That Declaration was read in cities and towns
To farmers, doctors, and ladies in fine gowns.
People cheered when Tom's words were read,
And they felt not fear, but fire instead.
Fire burned in their hearts for the chance to be free –
And that freedom was bought for you and for me.

So, remember next July 4th when the fireworks start,
And keep that memory close in your heart,
Of the man whose words created a nation,
Plus an annual celebration,
And think about Quill, that Founding Pup,
Who encouraged Tom when he almost gave up
Writing those words that can stir us still –
Those words he created with the help of a Quill!

- Kite -

(1776)

The fog was thick and the wind was cold
But Kite ran up the gangplank, as he'd been told.
Behind him, with boxes and trunks piled high,
Ben Franklin followed, and said with a sigh,
"Kite, my good fellow, this trip will be tough,
With lonely nights and seas often rough.
I've been appointed, this trip's not by chance,
To plead our cause before the King of France."

Just two weeks before, in a pleading call,
He'd been begged into service by one and all.
"Ben," said the Congress to this famous inventor
(Who was also a Patriot, sage, and printer),
"We've need of someone to seek aid for our fight,
Someone witty and wise, who'll make it seem right
That fighting the English is a worthy cause,
To gain our freedoms and make our own laws."

"So," said Ben, "On the morrow we sail,
When the sun comes up, and the sky's still pale.
Are you up for another adventure, my friend?
Will you stay by my side 'til the journey's end?"
Kite barked, "Yes!" for all to hear,
Causing the sailors to laugh and cheer,
As he ran in circles with obvious delight.
And those flying ears, which had named him Kite!

After weeks of sailing through wind and rain,
They landed in France, near the coast of Spain,
And they got in a carriage for a long, long ride,
To the city of Paris, where they would abide.
A city of flowers and artists galore,
A city that Ben would come to adore
Because of its beauty and the people he met,
Who came to love him, as well as his pet.

He dined at ten on escargot,
And everyone he got to know
Thought his plain brown clothes and beaver hat
Were utterly awesome, and so special that
He was the toast of the rich Paris elite,
And an evening with him was considered a treat.
People cheered for him wherever he went,
But he never forgot the reason he'd been sent.

Day after day he talked to the King,
Describing how ropes were pulled to ring
All the bells on the Fourth of July,
And how important it was that the French ally
Its ships and men with the U.S.A.,
And come to our aid without delay.
We'd need those ships and lots of men –
We'd need France to help us win!

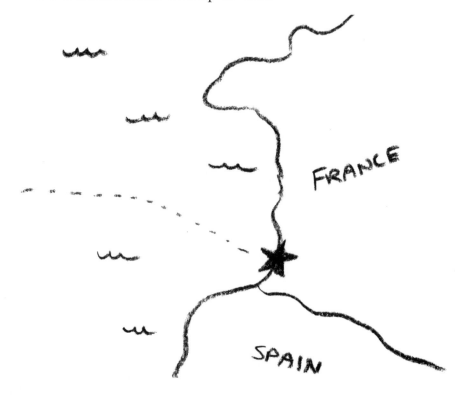

The King wouldn't decide to send guns or spend gold,
No matter how often Ben Franklin told
Him our men had few rifles and less lead,
Or even a blanket to make a bed.
Months dragged by while Kite and Ben
Begged that King, again and again.
And just when it seemed there was no help to get,
They met a young man named Lafayette.

This rich young man of noble birth
Felt the Patriots' cause was more than worth
What Franklin was asking the King of France,
And so he thought he'd take a chance
By going himself across the sea,
To offer his sword for liberty.
With a fond adieu for Ben and Kite,
Lafayette set sail to join our fight.

Yet, Ben and Kite felt their spirits wane
And they began to wonder if they'd ever gain
The ships and weapons they eagerly sought
To help the Patriots in the battles they fought.
But fate intervened on their side one day,
When Ben and Kite were playing croquet
With the King and others of the Royal Court,
Who enjoyed a day playing the sport.

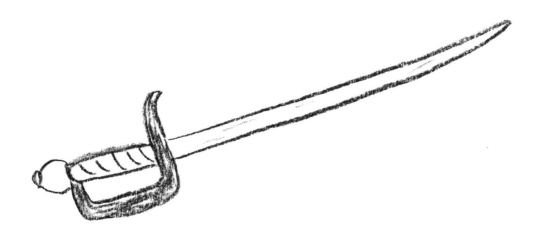

A courier arrived, and stashed deep in his pack
Was a message from Washington of an attack
Which ended in victory for the U.S.A.
And George hoped its contents would help to sway
The King into sending men and supplies,
So France and the U.S. would be certain allies.
"Your Majesty, may I speak with you now?"
Asked the courier politely, as he made a bow.

But before that courier could open his pack
The King hit the ball with a really loud WHACK!
It hit the courier, who tripped on a rake,
And dropped the pack, which got tossed toward the lake.
It soared through the air, but was stopped in mid-flight,
By a dog leaping high, who had ears like a kite!
He caught the pack with a bite of his teeth,
As he fell back down to the Earth beneath.

The King and Ben broke into applause
And cheered rather loudly for Kite, because
He had saved that message of great import,
That was sent to the King and his Royal Court.
If not for Kite, it would have been lost,
And oh the price it would surely have cost
Those Patriots who had sent Ben and Kite,
To plead for help with their ongoing fight.

But the King of France was so greatly impressed
With that victory, and also his guest,
That he sent lots of ships that very day
To sail really fast to the U.S.A.
Where they blocked British ships from the Yorktown coast,
Helping the Patriots burn the Redcoats like toast!
And it all came about because Ben and Kite
Kept on championing the Patriots' fight.

Kite and Ben were in Paris nine long years,
Helping our country, and hearing the cheers
Of people who honored the dog and the man
Who fought for our country when it first began.
They fought not with guns, but with words and pleas,
By leaving their home and crossing the seas.
This man and dog were Patriots all right –
A printer named Ben and a pup named Kite!

- *Rebel* -

(December 1775)

Rebel followed the General as he surveyed the camp.
His soldiers were hungry, cold, and damp.
The men were weary of fighting this war.
They longed for their families and homes afar.
It was Christmas Eve, and with no end in sight,
Of winning this war they all knew was right.
The General came up with what seemed a good plan,
To help revive the spirit deep in each man.

During the day the soldiers made ready,
Cleaning their guns with hands that were steady,
As they listened to orders for the coming night,
And what they should do to win the fight.
The General had planned a holiday surprise
Just at the dawning of the next sunrise.
The plan was clever, but posed danger for sure.
George knew that his troops had much to endure.

The Delaware River was icy and cold,
And on that Christmas night, so I've been told,
The General stood silently watching his men
Loading in boats for the crossing to begin.
The men were silent as he gave each a salute,
Then paused to pat the dog at his boot.
Rebel sensed danger, but stood ready to go,
Knowing his master would soon lead the show.

Rebel hopped in a boat at George's command
Going straight to the bow where he would stand,
As they crossed that freezing Delaware River,
To begin the march for the Patriots to deliver
A resounding blow to England's hired guns,
And prove the true grit of liberty's sons!
Yes, those tiny boats made a curious sight
As they crossed that river in the dead of night!

The fishermen who quietly tugged at the oars
Were careful and calm as they rowed from the shore.
Rebel glanced back at the men left behind,
And the blazing fires they'd continue to mind
So the enemy would think our camps fully manned,
Which was part of the deception the General had planned.
It was quite a bold venture, this crossing they made,
And Rebel was proud of the part that he played.

All was silence as each boat dropped the men
On the opposite shore, then rowed back again
For another load 'til all were across,
And each soldier delivered without a loss.
With Rebel at his side, George bravely led
That cold, biting march that the soldiers tread
To surprise those Hessians still snoozing away,
With no idea of the marching that day.

The march was freezing, the snow sometimes deep,
And many men had no boots for their feet,
So they wrapped them in rags, but still they bled –
Leaving the roadway with footprints of red.
This frigid path stung Rebel's poor paws,
But like a good soldier, he marched for the cause
And barked no complaint for any to hear,
As the Hessians' camp came ever so near.

Creeping upon the camp, their surprise was complete,
For those over-grogged soldiers were still fast asleep
And the Patriots' guns gave them no time or chance,
To grab up their weapons or put on their pants.
So into the cold in their long johns they ran
All in a dither, which had been George's plan!
There was screaming, and firing, and some tried to flee;
The smoke from the muskets made it hard to see.

Rebel kept guard of the General that day,
Who charged into battle and into harm's way.
George rode into battle, and never held back;
Always courageous, he led that attack!
And for years to come, Rebel would boast
Of his master's valor, far greater than most,
Which caused men to follow without doubt or fear,
And fight for the rights that they held so dear.

As the Hessians surrendered, the smoke blew away,
And it seemed that the battle was over that day.
But Rebel sensed danger was still lurking near,
So he glanced side to side, and then front to rear.
He spied a Hessian, who stopped as he fled,
To load up his musket with powder and lead,
Who then aimed at the General, and dropped to his knees,
To fire his musket with precision and ease.

But Rebel the Fearless sprang into action,
And in one tiny heartbeat, or merely a fraction,
He leaped at the horse who carried his master,
And the horse shot forward, averting disaster,
By spoiling the aim of that Hessian's lead
As it whizzed just to the side of Washington's head!
Then, pushing that enemy down in the dirt,
Rebel further made sure that George wasn't hurt.

The General hugged Rebel ever so tight,
And folded a blanket, and tied it just right
So Rebel could ride horseback, because
George knew the snow was hard on his paws.
So up went Rebel into this sling,
And off they raced, like a bird on the wing
To gather the troops and head for the river.
The crossing this time meant prisoners to deliver!

Riding with Rebel to the river that day,
The General was happy he'd found a way
To bring a victory to these strong, brave men,
Who followed his lead again and again.
And he was also glad that amid this strife,
Rebel had been close, and had saved his life.
Rebel's cunning, and courage, and loyalty, too,
Made him a Patriotic Pup, through and through!

- Lady Liberty -

(1777)

The plantation was gloomy, the weather was drear.
Martha stirred the fire as Liberty drew near.
"I'm lonely, Liberty, what about you?"
Said Martha to the dog, as she opened the flue.
"My George and your Rebel are so far away,
And I don't think I can stand it one more day!"
Wagging her tail, Liberty yipped she agreed,
Then Martha added, "I know what we need!"

Upstairs Martha scurried, with Liberty behind,
Where under the bed she knew she would find,
Bags and boxes, and a really large trunk,
Plus Liberty's chew toy, a sock that stunk!
She opened drawers, then to the closet she flew
Where she pulled out dresses – some old and some new.
She piled stockings and gloves all over the bed,
And those pretty little caps she wore on her head.

"Now, Liberty Girl, let's stop for some tea,
With biscuits for you and cookies for me.
We've much more to do to get ready to go;
We'll need to pack warmly for ice or snow.
The General and Rebel are in a new camp
That's near a river, where it's cold and damp.
Let's take a basket with a blanket, too,
To put by the fire for Rebel and you."

Their carriage traveled through mud and cold rain,
Avoiding the Redcoats, who hoped to gain
The General's wife as a captive, for trade.
A ransom for her would surely be made!
They could trade her for George, then hang him high,
As the King himself wanted George to die.
But her driver was careful, and made no mistakes,
Driving on the back roads, for all their sakes.

Arriving at Valley Forge in the dark of night,
Rebel barked loudly as they came into sight.
But what Martha had longed for mile after mile,
Was her husband's face that beamed with a smile,
When she ended that long and miserable ride,
And stepped from the carriage to be at his side.
"It's wonderful to see you, Martha, my dear,
And your comfort is needed by all who camp here."

She'd come to visit, and help in some way,
So she nursed sick soldiers, day after day.
Martha made medicine, and bandaged their hurts,
While Lady Liberty stayed close by at her skirts.
She cooked George's meals, and at night she would sew,
And as the storms brought freezing ice and snow,
Many more took sick for Martha to tend.
Oh, when would this war ever come to an end?

When Martha was helping the sick one night,
A wind extinguished her lantern light.
Her quarters with George were a half mile away,
And it was an easy walk when she left that day,
But it wouldn't be easy all alone,
With no light from the moon, or stars that shone.
And what would happen if she strayed from the camp?
Would she meet up with Redcoats as she tread through the damp?

Tripping and falling, she skinned her knee,
Then banged her head against a tree.
She couldn't remember which way to turn next,
Her thoughts were muddled, and her mind was vexed.
The howling wind increased her fright,
And no one could hear her calling that night.
The clouds opened up pouring icy rain,
Blinding her eyes, and increasing her pain.

But suddenly Martha heard sounds soft and sweet,
Of loving whimpers and pattering feet.
Liberty had been with Rebel that day,
When Martha had left to make her own way
Down to the huts where the sick lay abed,
And past the graves where others lay dead.
Yet, miraculously, Martha continued to hear
The sounds of Sweet Liberty as she came near.

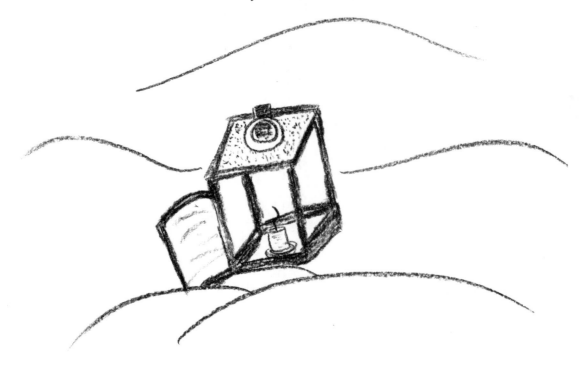

Liberty led Martha through the sleet and the snow,
Knowing exactly just how she should go
Through the dark of night at that Valley Forge farm,
Keeping her safe and free from harm.
"Liberty," said Martha, "You're such a treasure,
Bringing safety, and warmth, and always pleasure,
To those you love and those in need.
I'm glad I brought you, oh, yes indeed!"

As the ice on the river began to break,
George told Martha it was time to take
All the bags and boxes from under the bed,
And take Lady Liberty so that they could head
Back home to their lovely Mount Vernon plantation –
While he continued the fight to free our nation.
Watching them go would cause him to grieve,
But for their own safety he knew they must leave.

"Thank you for coming," said the General that day,
And he saluted them both as the coach rolled away.
"You're both brave soldiers who have served our cause,
Though one wears skirts and one has paws.
You have served with honor giving comfort and care.
You are both so special, my Patriotic Pair."
And off they rode toward home, and into history,
George Washington's wife, and her dog, Lady Liberty!

- The Legend Continues -

(Epilogue)

Christmas 1783

As the morning mist rose from the river
Peter quickened his steps as he sought to deliver
A Christmas surprise of such great import
That he stretched the stride of his legs stout and short.
The General and Rebel arrived late last night,
Home at last, from the long, weary fight.
The battles were over, and many lay dead,
But in the end, the General had lead
His troops to victory, and given a start
To the brand new nation so dear to his heart.
So just as the sun began to rise,
Peter hurried to spring this special surprise,
Which would chase the fatigue from the General's face,
And bring new joy to this wonderful place.

"Merry Christmas, Sir. Please come to the stable.
There's something you should see as soon as you're able."
So, hearing Peter's words, the General donned his cloak,
Whistling softly to Rebel, before Martha awoke.
And Lady Liberty followed close behind,
Knowing the General would surely not mind
If she tagged along to see what surprise lay ahead,
For the war weary soldier just up from his bed.
As the stable yard came into view,
Lady sensed the familiar, but also new.
George entered the stable, where inside a stall
Were crates tied with ribbons … four in all.
"Gifts," said Peter. "From friends far and wide.
Go ahead, Sir. See what's inside."

Lifting the lid from the crate on his right,
George gave a great laugh as his eyes caught sight
Of the wagging tail and the puppy face,
Beside a card which read, "We send you Chase.
This puppy is fearless, but also quite dear.
Season's Greetings from Beacon and Paul Revere!"
Lifting Beacon's son into his arms,
George was instantly smitten with the puppy's charms.
Around Chase's neck was a silver collar,
As shiny and bright as a brand new dollar!
Then, placing Chase in Liberty's care,
He moved to the next crate to see what was there.

The crate he saw next looked practically new,
All shiny and bright, painted red, white, and blue.
Curled on a blanket, in a pile of straw,
Was another pup with a card near his paw.
"Flag, funny fellow, is the image of his Pap,
He loves to play, and sit on your lap.
He bumps into things, and tracks mud in the hall.
He brings with him love and good tidings to all!"
Betsy Ross and Banner had sent Christmas cheer,
By sending Banner's son to live with him here.
But what awaited him in crate number three –
The one that smelled of the salt and the sea?

The crate was transported from France, via boat,
Arriving this morning with the following note:
"This mademoiselle has the name of Cherie,
And she is dearly loved by both Kite and me.
Kite is her Papa, and not by chance,
Her mother's the Poodle of The King of France!"
Congratulations on the end of our fight –
Happy Holidays, too, from Ben Franklin and Kite!"
And there in the crate, with manicured claws,
Was a dog whose ears gave George quite a pause.
They were covered with curls, but floppy and long;
With her Father's ears, she'd never go wrong!

The gift enclosed in crate number four,
Wiggled and squirmed when placed on the floor.
Around her neck was a card neatly tied,
And this was the message written inside:
"You've given hope to a nation brand new,
So, Hope is exactly what we send to you.
This daughter of Quill's is a darling lass,
And we couldn't let this holiday pass,
Without sending our sincerest wishes to you,
For a Merry Christmas and Happy New Year's, too!
And we pen words of praise for the victory you've won.
Your Friends, Quill, and Thomas Jefferson."

What a joyous Christmas at Mount Vernon plantation –
They'd won a war and the birth of a nation!
His Patriotic Pups had played a real part
In helping the nation get a good start.
Yet, he couldn't help wonder on that cold, Christmas morn,
About these new pups so recently born.
What rousing adventures for them lay ahead?
He knew that within them greatness was bred.
And what of him, this farmer who'd fought?
Greatness was something he'd never sought.
But, just for now, he'd put wonderings away,
And enjoy these new puppies so hard at play.
Chase, Flag, Hope, and little Cherie,
Were chasing each other all around a tree!

They hadn't a thought of a nation or cause,
Only running and jumping with big puppy paws.
Their parents and grandparents were Patriots all,
And if, in the future, their country should call,
They'd stand with the General, and serve the new nation,
But today was a day of celebration,
Of family, and friends, and freedom, too –
With tails to chase, and bones to chew.
So the rowdy pups made the General smile,
With their puppy ways and beagle style.
Like those first Founding Pups of Mount Vernon plantation,
Their place at Mount Vernon brought real jubilation,
And the General was sure as each one grew up,
That each would become a Patriotic Pup!

- The Truth of the Tales -

The Truth of the Tales

The Legend Begins

Mount Vernon was a working plantation, and the cherished home of George and Martha Washington. George raised all sorts of farm animals, including many litters of dogs. He especially loved hunting dogs because, as an excellent horseman himself, he often hosted foxhunts at Mount Vernon. For many years, he had a stable master named Peter, who would have certainly been involved with any litter of new pups.

In 1775, the Continental Congress named George Washington as Commander in Chief of the Continental Army. He left Mount Vernon to lead the fight for freedom, and did not return home until Christmas Eve, 1783.

Beacon

Late at night on April 18, 1775, Paul Revere left his silversmith's shop in Boston to ride through the countryside, warning the citizens that the British were marching toward Lexington to seize their weapons. During this ride, he was captured by British soldiers, but later released without his horse. He managed to return to Lexington and later fled to safety, along with other patriots, John Hancock and Sam Adams, also being sought by the British, who considered them traitors. When the British marched into Lexington on April 19, the minutemen were waiting for them at the Village Green. Nobody is certain who fired that first shot at Lexington, but it is often called "the shot heard 'round the world" because the fight for freedom began with that first shot.

Banner

In 1776, Betsy Ross was the struggling widow of a Continental soldier. She had an upholstery business and also earned extra money doing all sorts of sewing. She often told her children and grandchildren the story of how surprised she was one evening when she received a visit from General Washington and two other members of a secret committee from the Continental Congress. During that visit, the General showed her the sketch of a flag with a six-pointed star. Expertly using her scissors, Betsy demonstrated to the Committee how to make a five-pointed star with only one snip. The men were impressed with her skill, and convinced her to create the first flag for the Continental Army. Working at night, Betsy completed that original flag at the beginning of June, 1776, and on June 14, 1777, the Continental Congress adopted our national flag of 13 stars in a field of blue, with 13 alternating red and white stripes to represent the original 13 colonies.

Quill

July 4, 1776 is considered the birthday of the United States of America because, on that day, the Declaration of Independence was adopted. Riders took copies all across the thirteen colonies, where it was read aloud that day in town squares for all the people to hear. Thomas Jefferson had been chosen to write this document, and he had worked on it in a small house near The Pennsylania State House where the Congress met. After he completed writing it, it was debated, discussed, and revised during several weeks, before a vote was finally taken to adopt it. Since that July 4th, Americans have celebrated with fireworks and festivities. The Pennsylvania State House, in Philadelphia, is now called Independence Hall in honor of the great document that was adopted there by the Continental Congress.

Kite

Although the French believed that a patriot victory would benefit their country by weakening their enemies, the British, the French refused to openly support the United States until they proved themselves in battle. The Congress sent Benjamin Franklin to France to seek their help because he was the most famous American at that time. Although he was quite popular with everyone in France, it was not until word arrived of an American victory that money and troops were finally sent. By 1780, there were 5,500 soldiers from France in the United States. In late September 1781, American troops, aided by the French, surrounded British General Cornwallis near Yorktown, Pennsylvania, and French ships blocked their retreat on Chesapeake Bay. On October 19, 1781, the British surrendered to General Washington as the band played and young French General Lafayette, who had volunteered to help in our fight, joyfully watched.

Rebel

By Christmas of 1776, George Washington and his discouraged troops had withdrawn to New Jersey. On that bitterly cold Christmas night, Washington ordered about 2,400 men to cross the Delaware River. They were safely rowed across by New England lobstermen and fishermen who expertly navigated the floating ice. Washington left behind a few men to keep campfires burning so that the enemy across the river would not suspect such a crossing was in progress. After making the dangerous trip across the river, Washington and his troops began a cold, nine-mile march to surprise the Hessians, hired German troops fighting for the British. The march through snow and icy conditions was horrible for the men, many of whom had wrapped their feet in rags because they had no shoes for their feet. The road became covered with bloody footprints as they silently marched. The early morning attack totally surprised the enemy soldiers, who were sleeping after a night of holiday celebrating. They ran out of their shelters attempting to put on their uniforms and gather in fighting formation. Washington and his men were able to capture more than 900 soldiers and many weapons. This victory helped to raise the spirits of the Patriots, giving them hope that they might actually defeat the British. It also further spread the nickname the British had given to Washington: "The Fox!"

Lady Liberty

Despite the fact that his huge responsibilities prevented General Washington from returning to Mount Vernon during the war, Martha attempted to visit him whenever the troops were camped somewhere for extended periods of time. In December of 1777, his army was quartered on a farm at Valley Forge, Pennsylvania. The troops were plagued with a serious shortage of food, shoes, and warm clothing. Although many died of sickness that winter, Martha did all she could to ease their suffering. She brewed homemade medicines and spent countless hours tending the sick. Her gentle acts of mercy provided the homesick and ill troops with encouragement and endurance to continue the fight to bring freedom to our new nation.

☆ THE END ☆

Glossary

abide (ə·bīd´) v. to live in a place

adieu (ə·dū´) n. farewell

ally (ə·lī´) v. to form a connection between

amid (ə·mĭd´) prep. in or into the middle of

averting (ə·vûrt´·ing) v. to keep from happening

cloak (klōk) n. a long loose outer garment

contemplation (kŏn´·təm·plā´·shən) n. the act of thinking about something for a long time

croquet (krō·kā´) n. a game in which players drive wooden balls with mallets through a series of wickets set out on a lawn

cunning (kən´·ing) adj. skillful and clever at using special knowledge or at getting something done

deception (di·sep´·shən) n. the act of causing someone to believe what is not true

delegated (del·ə·gāt·ed) v. appointed

donned (dŏnd) v. put on

drear (drir) adj. without cheer, gloomy

elite (i·lēt´) n. those thought of as the best people

endure (en·dūr´) v. to hold out

escargot (es·kår·gō´) n. French a snail served as food

grieve (grēv) v. to be very sad

hunch (hunch) n. a feeling or suspicion you don't have reason for

ignited (ig·nīt´·ed) v. to set on fire

keen (kēn) adj. strong

mellow (mĕl´·ō) adj. soft

pleas (plēs) n. requests

rowdy (rou´·dē) adj. rough, disorderly

silversmith (sil´·vər·smith´) n. a person who makes items of silver

smitten (smit´·ən) adj. suddenly and strongly affected

steed (stēd) n. a horse

throng (thrông) n. a crowd

treason (trē´·zən) n. the act of being false to one's country

vexed (vekst) adj. annoyed

Bibliography

Historical facts were gathered from the following sources:

1. The World Book Encyclopedia, Volume 16, World Book, Inc.

2. George Washington web site:
http://www.nps.gov/history/nr/travel/delaware/was.htm

3. Martha Washington web sites:
http://ap.grolier.com/article?assetid=atb999b204&templatename=/article/article.html
http://www.history.org/Almanack/people/bios/biomwash.cfm
http://www.ushistory.org/betsy/flagtale.html

4. Betsy Ross web site:
http://www.ushistory.org/betsy/flagtale.html

5. Thomas Jefferson web site:
http://www.ushistory.org/declaration/graff.htm

6. Benjamin Franklin web site:
http://sln.fi.edu/franklin/timeline/timeline.html

7. Paul Revere web site:
http://www.paulreverehouse.org/ride/real.shtml

Kids' Comments

"*Patriotic Pups* is a really good book. I would love a companion like a patriotic pup. I would recommend this book: ***** the best. I love this book!"
—Natasha, Third Grade

"I would recommend this book to anyone. It is terrific. I hope you love this book."
—Madison, Third Grade

"Absolutely, positively five star. Kids will love this Historical Fiction book of one of their favorite animals: Dogs. So find out what happens to the patriotic pups."
—Jack, Third Grade

"*Patriotic Pups* was so fun to read."
—Miranda, Third Grade

"I think you should read this book because it is very fun."
—Anila, Third Grade

"I would recommend this book for people who like to laugh. It was a great book. You will love it."
—Harrison, Third Grade

"Mount Vernon was the happiest place. Hopefully you will be inspired by this book review and read this book and be as excited as ever."
—Lauren, Third Grade

"I recommend *Patriotic Pups* to other people because it is a very good story."
—Tommy, Third Grade

"My favorite pup is Kite, and his master is Ben Franklin. Kite's part is about when Kite and Ben Franklin go to France and ask for more soldiers. So when you read the book *Patriotic Pups* read about Kite."
—Kylie, Third Grade

"I thought it was a very good book. You should read it because it would be very interesting to you. Once you read it you will know how good the book really is."
— Cody, Third Grade

"If you like rhyming books you'll love this book too!"
— Analisa, Third Grade

"I like the adventure of all the pups. They're funny. That makes you smile."
— Kelcie, Third Grade

"I think Betsy Ross and Banner were the best part in the story because I learned that Betsy had to sew the flag in the basement because Red Coats were right outside."
— Sydnee, Third Grade

Patriotic Pups

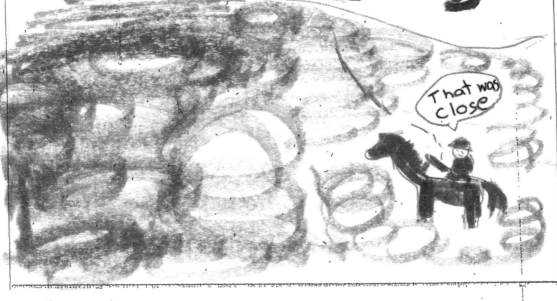

Rebel knocking down
a hessian.

Patriotic Pups

Banner & BetsyRoss

Patriotic Pups

Beacon

Patriotic Pups

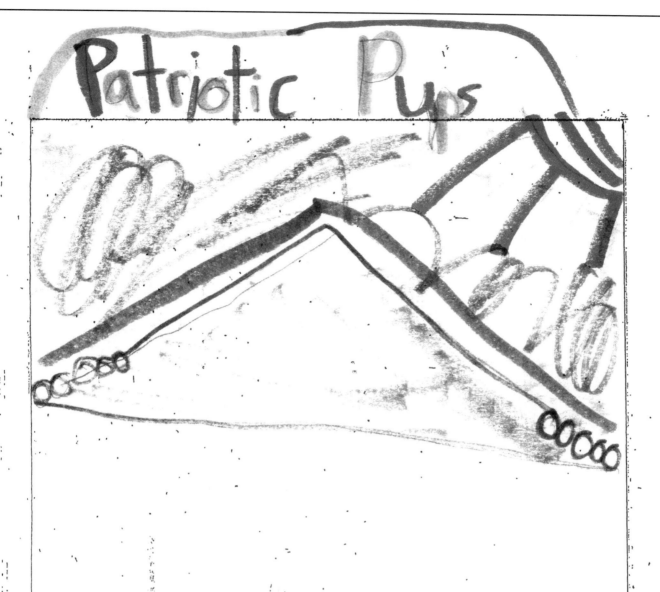

Lady Liberty

Teachers' Comments

"Wow, what a wonderful piece of literature for the classroom! I especially like how each Patriotic Pup has his own chapter. This will allow for a great introduction into a breakdown for each important historical Patriot into a lesson. I also like the continuation of the story along with the use of "The Truth of the Tales" section at the end of the book. It was a nice way to tie the fictional history into its non-fictional counterpart. I cannot wait to use this wonderful book as an added addition and teaching tool in my classroom."
—Jessica Tosh, Fifth Grade Teacher

"I am thoroughly enchanted with *Patriotic Pups*! What a wonderful way to introduce children to American History! Our program uses a rhyming component for instruction. *Patriotic Pups* is an excellent example of this writing technique."
—DyAnne Shultz, Retired Teacher, currently consulting with ABC Phonetic Reading School, Inc. (NCLB)